# DIARY OF A MINECRAFT ZOMBIE

# BOOK 12

# PiXELMON GONE

# DIARY OF A MINECRAFT ZOMBIE

## BOOK 12

# PIXELMON GONE

## BY

## Zack Zombie

# TUESDAY

"ZACKARY JULIUS ZOMBIE! YOU GET DOWN HERE RIGHT NOW!!!"

Oh, boy, what did I do now?

"Look at this!"

"Look at what?"

"Look at these dishes! You were supposed to do your CHORES hours ago!"

All I kept hearing from my mom's mouth was BLAH, BLAH, BLAH, BLAH.

"So, what's the big deal?"

"Humph! Zackary Julius Zombie, don't you give me lip, young man!"

"But Zombies don't have lips."

"Don't you get smart with me!"

"Duh, otay, I'll just act reel dum," I said.

## BAD MOVE.

"I have a mind to ground you and take away all your video games for a month if you don't start doing these dishes right now!"

"I don't care. Chores are stupid!"

"WHA. . .? You take that back right now or you're grounded for the rest of your life! No video games, no sleepovers, and NO CAKE!"

Oh, man! She pulled out the heavy guns.

## NOT FAIR.

Now, what am I gonna do? I mean, I can't live without videogames, I can't live without my friends and I definitely can't live without cake!

But I can't give in. Every kid in Minecraft World is counting on me.

I can't let my mom win or every kid in the Minecraft World will be forever enslaved to the whims of their parent overlords.

But, I just kept hearing those fatal words echoing in my big skull. . .

"NO-NO-NO-NO-NO. . .CAKE-CAKE-CAKE-CAKE-CAKE!"

I'm sorry, brothers. . .I just don't have the strength to sacrifice it all for the sake of the cause.

Wow, Zombie life is **SO CRUEL.** . .

"All right, Mom. I take it back. . ."

"And the dishes?"

"I'll do them later. . ."

"No, you need to dirty these dishes right now or no video games and no cake," she said.

Man, she's hardcore.

"Okay, Mom, I'll dirty the dishes."

HHAACCKK! SPLAT, HHAACCKK! SPLAT,
HHAACCKK! SPLAT!

## "DISHES DONE."

"Wait a minute, you missed a spot."

UUURRRGGHH!

HHAACCKK! SPLAT!

"All right, can I go now?!!"

"See, that wasn't so hard now, was it?"

UUURRRGGHH. . .

"Now, don't you want a little piece of
cake?" she said with her triumphant,
smug smile.

What can I say. . .I'm weak.

So much for standing up for the **OPPRESSED** kids of the world.

Please don't judge me.

CHOMP, CHOMP, CHOMP. . .
Shame. . . CHOMP.

# WEDNESDAY

"Zombie."

Clickety Clack, Clickety Clack, Clickety Clack. . .

"Zombie."

**CLICKETY CLACK,** Clickety Clack, Clickety Clack. . .

"Zombie!"

Clickety Clack, Clickety Clack, Clickety Clack. . .

"ZOMBIE!"

Clickety Clack, Clickety Clack, Clickety Clack. . .

YANK! ZZZTT!

"Hey! What'd you that for?!!! I was having the perfect game?!"

"Zombie, why didn't you bring in the garbage?"

**"THE GARBAGE?!!** DAD! You stopped my perfect game for that?!!"

"Zombie, you promised to bring in the garbage," my dad said.

I don't know where parents get their information. But, somehow, they're all convinced that we kids signed a contract somewhere saying that we were going to actually do chores around the house.

"No, I didn't! I never said I would bring in the garbage."

"Zombie, you said if I gave you five more minutes you would finish your game and bring in the garbage. That was thirty minutes ago."

"I never said that."

*Or if I did say it, I* **DEFINITELY** *didn't mean it.*

"Well, bring in the garbage."

"You're the worst!"

"Zombie, don't mouth off and do as you're told!"

I looked down to see if I dropped my mouth again. It happens sometimes you know. . .it's a Zombie thing.

"Zombie, stop trying to be **SMART.**"

"Duh, otay, I'll just be reel dum," I said.

Bad move.

"THAT'S IT! You're grounded for a month! No video games, no sleepovers and no CAKE!"

UURRRGGHHH! They got me again!

Man, as long as my parents **CONTROL** my triad of excitement, I have to obey their every whim.

I've got to find a way to break these bonds of slavery and get my freedom.

But what can I do? They control all the valuable resources.

Plus, I wouldn't even know how to make my own cake.

But, if I could get control of all the resources, I thought, I could rise and help all the children in Minecraft World to **OVERTHROW** their Parental Masters and reek our revenge on parents all over the world. . . MUAHAHAHAHAHA!

"You know I can hear you, right?"

What the what?!!

That's the problem with having holes in your head.

Look out garbage, here I come.

# ☀ THURSDAY ✳

"ZOMBIE, DID YOU FINISH YOUR HOMEWORK?" my mom yelled from downstairs.

But for some reason all I heard was, "Zombie, BLAH, BLAH, BLAH, BLAH!"

I didn't have time for distractions anyway because I was about to get to the **BOSS LEVEL** on my favorite game—Zombie's Duty, Black Ops 3—Human Edition.

Yeah, I know. Blasting humans is not the nicest thing to do. Especially for six hours straight. And it will probably lead to increased aggressive behavior, low attention span and anti-social tendencies. . .

But, it's still awesome!

Take that, you human **MEATBAGS!** URRRGGHH!

"ZOMBIE! BLAH, BLAH, BLAH, BLAH!" my mom yelled again.

There she goes again! Man, can't she see that I'm saving the world from the human plague that is threatening all Zombiedom!

**TAKE THAT!** URRRRGGHH!

YES! I FINALLY MADE IT! I'M AT THE BOSS ROUND! SO, I CAN'T MESS THIS UP. . .

Suddenly, my mom burst into the room.

"ZOMBIE, don't ignore me! I asked you if you finished your homework?!!"

Again, all I heard was, "ZOMBIE, BLAH, BLAH, BLAH, BLAH!"

"No, Mom. I'm not hungry right now, thanks anyway. . .take that, you human meat puppet! URRRRGGHH!"

"Zombie, I **WARNED** you. . ."

YANK! ZZZTT!

"WHAT THE WHAT?!!!"

"NNNNOOOOOOOO!!!!"

Then, all I could see was my mom standing there holding the power cord to my game console.

It felt more like she just tore out my heart and was holding it in Mortal Kombat triumph.

All I could hear was, "**FINISH HIM!**"

"Zombie, I'm sorry I had to disconnect your video game, but I need to know if you've finished your homework and. . ."

"WWWWWWWWAAAAHHHHH!!!!!"

"Zombie, it's just a video game. Stop crying and answer my question."

"But, Mom, whose gonna save the Zombie race from the human infestation that has descended upon it? WAAAAAAAAHHHH!!!!"

"Zombie, **STOP** that right now! If you don't finish your homework by the time I get back, you're not getting this back." Then, she tore out the rest of my console along with all my important organs that were connected to it.

And as she walked out the door, I slowly saw my thirteen-year-old life flash before my eyes. Then, everything went black.

Thirty minutes later. . .

"Zombie, get your head out of the trash can and start doing your homework," the prison guard said.

This was my life now. I was on year thirteen of an eighteen-year prison sentence. Every move I made was under constant **SURVEILLANCE.** And I could only get privileges if I completed my hard labor.

And if I didn't listen, I got thrown in the hole. . .solitary confinement with no video games, no friends and no cake.

I don't know if I'm gonna make it.

It's either gonna do me in or I need to. . .I need to. . .

That's it! I need to escape!

No one that has tried to escape this **PARENTAL DEATH TRAP** has ever been seen again.

But I need to succeed where my brothers in arms have failed.

I had to make a Prison Break!

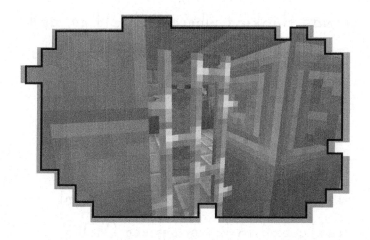

# FRIDAY

That's it. Today's the day.

Today is the day I'm going to **ESCAPE** my parents' iron grip and taste the sweet flavor of freedom.

Today is the day I'm running away.

I was thinking where I should go, and I thought the best **PLACE** would be to run away to the jungle biome and live with the animals.

I saw a movie about a Zombie that was raised by gorillas once. He looked pretty cool in his one-piece Ocelot skinned outfit. Especially when he would swing from tree to tree yelling at the top of his lungs.

"UUURRRGGHHUUURRRGGGHHHUU-URRRGGHHH!"

He lived in a hut **IN A TREE** all by himself, and his animal friends.

That just sounded so cool, I had to do it.

I started thinking about all my friends and how much I would miss them.

But, I couldn't let that stop me. I had to take a stand for all the Minecraft Kids and the oppression they faced.

And I knew once I had trained all the animals to follow my psychic commands, I would come back with my **ANIMAL ARMY** and rescue all the kids in Minecraft.

At least that's how the Zombie in the movie did it.

I couldn't bring much, but I took everything I would need to survive in the jungle.

I snuck my video game console from my mom's favorite hiding place.

Yes,' I thought. I can finally save the Zombie race from the Human pestilence!

And, don't worry, I'm not dumb. I made sure to remember to bring all the **POWER CORDS** for my video game console.

I took my dad's cell phone to stay in touch with Steve and the guys, and I took my mom's recipe for cake. Yeah, I ate the last piece of cake last night so I had to figure out how to make it from scratch.

But that's okay. I'm resourceful.

And if Zarzan, Lord of the Jungle Biome could do it, so can I.

Sweet Freedom, here I come!

"UUUURRRGGHHUUURRRGGGHHUU-
URRRGGHHH!"

# SATURDAY

So. . . I'm back home today.

Yeah, things didn't turn out like I expected.

Well, the closest **JUNGLE** was the Jungle biome amusement park which was a few miles away from my house.

I thought it would be the perfect place.

But the security guards didn't think so.

Took me a few hours, but I finally lost them.

And I found the best tree to build
**MY HUT**.

I tried to get a bunch of tree branches
to build it, but I couldn't find any good
ones.

So, finally, I tried to punch a tree like
Steve does.

Now I realize why Zombies don't punch
trees.

After that, it was really hard building
my tree hut with only one arm.

But it was okay, I thought, I'll just
use my **PSYCHIC POWERS** and
get some gorillas to do all the work.

So, I found a few gorillas in a cage at the amusement park and stared at them for a few minutes to make sure they got my **INSTRUCTIONS.**

Then I opened the cage and nodded at them in agreement.

I don't remember much after that. . .

But boy it was really hard finding my legs.


I tried to take my mind away from things, so I pulled out my video game console to finish my Zombie's Duty, Black Ops 3—Boss fight.

Yeah, that didn't go well.

Then I thought I would call Steve and the guys to let them know how I was doing.

But, for some reason the phone wouldn't turn on.

I don't get it. My dad used it all day yesterday. Why wasn't it **WORKING** now?

And I really, really needed it.

Especially when the sun came up.

Ouch. . .

So here I am, back home again.

And the **SCHOOL PRINCIPAL** called my house and told my mom and dad that I skipped school.

So not only am I in extreme pain. . .

But, I got no video games. . .

I got no friends. . .

And I got no cake.

Man, Zombie kid life is cruel.

# ☀ SUNDAY ☀

Today, I went to see Steve.

I was thinking maybe he could help me escape the PARENT TRAP.

Steve's got it good, you know.

You see, he doesn't have parents.

He said that some Villagers found him in the Forest Biome when he was a little kid.

So growing up, Steve didn't really have anybody to tell him what to do, and where to go, and what to eat, and how to dress, and to do his homework, and to stop playing video games, and when to go to bed, and how to behave, and to do chores, and to stop watching so much TV, and to go to school, and. . .

Wow. . .Steve's got it **REALLY GOOD.**

Even though Steve is a little weird.

Like when he punches trees. . .

Or when he eats raw pork chops. . .

Or like when he only uses one hand to do everything.

And then he shakes people's hand. . . with the same hand.

So nasty.

But man, he's got the life.

I mean, I can only **IMAGINE** what life would be like without my parents. I would be free to do whatever I want.

I can play video games 24/7.

I can eat cake all day.

I wouldn't have to go to school and never ever have to do homework.

I can dress whatever way I want. . . no more turquoise shirts and blue pants, yeah!

I can hang out with my friends every day, even on a school night.

I can even brush my teeth and take a bath once in a while. . .

Wow, that would be the life.

But who am I **KIDDING?**

I'm gonna be under my parents' iron grip forever, and there's no way out.

I might as well get used to wearing an orange jumpsuit. . .

With blue pants, of course.

I found Steve, and he was at his new house right outside the Human Village.

He just finished building his new house because a gang of Street Kids **BLEW UP** his old house a few days ago.

Yeah, some Street Kids recently started causing all kinds of trouble around the neighborhood when the orphanage up the hill closed.

My mom said that the orphan kids cause a lot of trouble because they don't have any place to go. She said they're really lonely, so they take their frustration out on society.

She even said that if they had good role models, it would help them learn to be respectable and responsible adults.

PFFFTT! Yeah, dumb, I know.

I don't know how **ROLLING** is going to help them be more respectable and responsible.

"Yo, Steve, wassup?"

"Nothin', wassup with you?

"Nothin', wassup with you?"

"Nothin', wassup with you?"

"Err. . .nothing, how's the new house coming?" I asked.

"Good," Steve said. "This time I'm building my house out of **STONE** so those crazy kids can't blow it up."

"Whoa, that's cool."

"Yeah, my first house was made of dirt, and they blew that one up; my second house was built out of wood, and they blew that up so now I'm using stone."

"Good idea. Hey, why are those kids bothering you anyway?" I asked.

"I don't know. I found one of them a few weeks ago and I helped him out. He was a spider named Nate that had flipped over and couldn't get back up. So, I helped him out and then he started following me around everywhere."

"Whoa."

"Next thing you know, his friends started following me around everywhere too. And there's a bunch of them: there's spiders, creepers, zombies, skeletons, endermen, shulkers, silverfish, slimes. . .and there's even a **HUMAN KID** named Jeb."

"What do they want?"

"I don't know, they just kept following me around. Then they started sleeping next to my house. One day, I came home from mining Diamonds and I think I surprised them. Next thing you know, I had to build a new house."

"Really?"

"Yeah, and while I was building the new house, they started **GATHERING** wood blocks for me and helping me out."

"That's cool."

"Yeah, it was really cool, but I don't know if anybody ever taught them how to build stuff. Because one of the creepers leaned against one of the walls and then the whole thing fell down. . . Then, it blew up. . .or was it the other way around? Heh, I forgot."

"Wow. Where are the kids now?"

"I don't know. They just stopped coming. I thought maybe they found a new home. But I kinda' miss them you know. . . especially little Nate; he was cool."

"Yeah, I get that. . .sorry, bro."

"No worries. So, what's up with you, Zombie? How's life at the **ZOMBIE HOUSE?** Your mom make any cake lately? I could really use a bite right now. Nobody makes cake like your mom does."

"Sorry, man, ate the last piece for breakfast," I said.

"Bummer. Man, it sure beats eating potatoes and mushroom stew. That's all I ever eat around here."

"Stew? Yuck, I hate that stuff."

"Yeah, that's all Villagers know how to make, so potatoes and stew for breakfast,  potatoes and stew for lunch, they even make stewed potatoes for dinner," Steve said.

"**WHOA**. . .that's cold, bro."

"Yeah, they serve it cold too. . ."

Nasty. I thought.

"So, you looked like you wanted to ask me something," Steve said. "What's up?"

I totally forgot what I came to ask, Steve. All I kept thinking about was life without cake.

**THE HORROR!** I shuttered just thinking about it.

"Forget it, man. It isn't a big deal," I said. "But I'll see you later. Good luck on your new house."

So, as I was leaving, a bell rang from the village. I could tell from Steve's long face that it was dinnertime.

Potatoes and stew.

Nasty.

Wow. Life with **NO CAKE...**

Man, that must be rough.

# M✷NDAY

At school today, all the kids were crowding around this one kid that had brought his pet to school for show and tell.

Except it wasn't a wolf or an ocelot or a squid, or anything like that.

It was **STRANGE ANIMAL** called a Pixelmon.

"What is that?!!!" the kids started yelling.

"Where did you get it?!!!!"

"Hey, I want one!!!!"

"Now, kids, settle down," Ms. Bones said. "Let Ichabod tell you more about his pet."

The kid's name was Ichabod. He was a Skeleton exchange student from some place called Woodland Manor. So he had a weird accent and drank a **LOT OF TEA.**

He was kind of a snob, too. It was just weird how he stuck out his pinky a lot.

I met him once, on the first day of school. It was in the cafeteria while he was drinking tea.

Me and the guys went over to him to introduce ourselves.

"Hi, I'm Zack, but you can call me Zombie," I said, reaching for a high-five.

He just **LOOKED** at me, then looked at my hand, then he looked at me again like I had eaten somebody's brains or something.

"Humph! Well my name is Ichabod Percival Freely. I am of the Woodland Freely Royal Family, thirteenth generation on my mother's side," he said as he rolled his eyes. . .

Yeah, I know. . .Skeleton's don't have eyes. But I if he did, I bet he was rolling them at me right then.

"But my friends call me I.P.," he said with a smug look. . .and with his pinky still sticking out.

"PFFFTTT!" Skelee said as he burst out laughing.

"What's so funny?" Ichabod demanded.

"Your name is I.P. Freely?" Skelee said.

Then we all looked at each other and then we burst out **LAUGHING.**

Ichabod just looked at us like we spit in his lunch or something and stormed away.

"What's up with that guy?" Skelee asked.

"I don't know," I said. "Probably had to go to the bathroom."

Then, we all burst out laughing, again.

"Yo, Zombie, you should probably put your hand down," Skelee said.

"Oh, yeah. . ."

So much for being cool.

But today, Ichabod was the most popular kid in school. All because he brought his **PIXELMON PET** to school.

"WHERE CAN I GET ONE?!!!" the kids just kept screaming and yelling in excitement.

"Unfortunately," Ichabod said, "unless you have a lot of money like my family does, you cannot buy one. You will have to go out to the Forest Biome and catch one like the common folk do," he said as he looked down on all of us. . . and I bet he rolled his eyes again.

"Thank you, Ichabod," Ms. Bones interrupted. "Please take your seat."

It seemed like Ichabod **FLOATED** over to his seat with his Pixelmon around his shoulders and with his little pinky sticking out.

"Don't worry, kids," Ms. Bones said. "I have a friend who is a professor, who studies Pixelmon. I'm sure he would be happy to let us visit his lab on a school field trip. Then we could learn more about Pixelmon up close."

"YEAHHHHHHH!!!!!" all the kids yelled.

But I have to admit, I got really excited too. I wanted my own Pixelmon. I wanted a Pixelmon I could **TRAIN** and call my own.

But I didn't want to wait to go on the field trip to wait to see one.

I need to go out to the forest and catch one myself. Or maybe two, or three, or twelve?!!!

When I looked around, I could tell that all the other kids had the same idea.

So, it would be a race to see who could catch the most Pixelmon.

And at that moment, I decided to devote my life to being a **PIXELMON MASTER.**

Pixelmon World, get ready cause I am going to become the greatest Pixelmon Master ever!

# TUESDAY

"AAAAAAAHH!!!"

"Zombie, what is **THAT?!!!**" my mom yelled.

"It's a Pixelmon. I found it on my way home from visiting Dad at the Nuclear Waste Plant. It was just lying there in some green ooze in the swamp behind the plant."

"Are you sure that thing is okay?" my mom asked. "Why does it look so fleshy and pink?"

My mom had a point. It didn't look anything like the Pixelmon that

Ichabod had brought to school. This one had short stubby ears, a really weird tail, no hair, and it drooled a lot.

. . .Looked kinda like one of **STEVE'S BABY** pictures.

"Mom, he's fine. And he's gonna be my new pet," I said.

"Zombie, I'm worried," my mom said. "That thing doesn't look sanitary. I don't know if I feel safe having that thing in the house."

"Please, Mom. I'll take care of it. I PROMISE!"

Then, my Pixelmon jumped out of my arms and started to rub itself on my mom's leg.

"Eeeeewwww! Get it away from me. Get it away. Get it away!" Mom said, cringing.

Then all of a sudden, ZZZZAAAPPPP!!!!!

My mom started shining like a bright Christmas tree. Then everything smelled like rotten flesh.

"Owwwww!" she yelled.

Whoa, my Pixelmon can control **LIGHTNING!** That's AWESOME!

Except my mom didn't think so. She started turning red and then it really started smelling like rotten flesh in the house.

I got my cue and ran out of the house with my Pixelmon. There was no way my mom was going to let me keep him now. So, I'm going to have to hide him, at least until the rotten flesh smell goes away.

So, I ran to the shed and made a little bed for him out of newspaper.

But, wow! My Pixelmon can generate electricity. I wonder what else he could do.

A-chu, A-chu, A-chu!

All of a sudden, my Pixelmon started **SNEEZING.** Guess he didn't like the cold.

So, I got an old blanket from the shed and wrapped him in it.

So, what am I going to call you?

I looked him over and tried think about a few **NAMES**.

How about Fleshy? Or Pinky? Or maybe Rigley?

A-chu, A-chu, A-chu!

Naaah! Those are lame.

How about Bolt? It was so cool how you generated that lightning bolt!

A-chu, A-chu, A-chu!

Naah! Not cool enough.

How about Steve?

A-chu, A-chu, A-chu!

Naah! Steve would probably get mad at me or something.

I just sat there thinking. . .

A-chu, A-chu, A-chu!

"Man, you're really cold." So I wrapped him up a bit tighter in the blanket.

Then it hit me. . .

I got it! How about Pixel-chu!

Next thing I know. . .
ZZZZAAAAAAPPP!!!!

Yeah. . .I think he likes it.

So, there he is, my new Pixelmon. . . Pixelchu!

I held him and I was so proud of my Pixelmon.

"You and me are going to be **BEST FRIENDS** forever, Pixelchu!"

I think he smiled because his little pink face got all wrinkly and then. . .

ZZZZAAAAAAPPP!!!!

Hey!

ZZZZAAAAAAPPP!!!!

Owww!

ZZZZAAAAAAPPP!!!!

Hey, stop that!

ZZZZAAAAAAPPP!!!!

ZZZZAAAAAAPPP!!!!

ZZZZAAAAAAPPP!!!!

# WEDNESDAY

"Zombie, hurry up and get ready. The school bus is leaving in a few minutes," my mom yelled from downstairs.

So I ran downstairs, really excited to tell the guys at school about Pixelchu.

I had **HIDDEN** Pixelchu in my bag, and I was hoping to sneak out before my mom saw him.

I was also really excited about our field trip to visit Ms. Bones' Professor friend at the Pixelmon lab today. I wanted to learn everything there is to know about Pixelmon.

"See you later, Mom," I said, running out of the house.

"Zombie, stop right there," she said.

Oh, man. . .I'm **CAUGHT.**

What happened to you?" she asked. "You look a bit crispy this morning."

"Uuuhh. . ."

"And have you been using your dad's Rotten Flesh cologne again?" she asked. "Zombie, you know that cologne is very expensive. And I got it for your father to use for special occasions."

"Uh. . .Yeah, sorry, Mom. You see, there's this girl at school, and. . ."

"Ooooooh! Zombie, you have a new crush, hmmm?" she said with her mom face.

I always know that if I ever need to distract my mom, I just have to bring up girls.

"Yeah. . .but I gotta go!" I said running out of the house.

Phew! **MADE IT.**

That was so close.

Pixelchu was moving around, so I thought maybe he was getting tired of being stuffed in my bag.

So, I opened it up to give him some fresh air.

ZZZZAAAAAAPPP!!!!

Yeah. . .he didn't like that.

When we got to the Professor's lab, it was a big building with huge antennas poking up from the top.

Looked like the kinda place where they would do **EXPERIMENTS** on Humans and kick start the next Human Apocalypse.

Yeah, they probably have a bunch of rotten flesh eating Humans in the basement, just waiting for an unsuspecting group of kids to come visit so they could have their next meal. . .

I think I've been playing too many video games.

Anyway, we met the Zombie Professor, who was really nice. He said his name was Professor Spruce, like the tree.

But we just couldn't wait to see the Pixelmon.

Then, he took us into a **BIG ROOM** with small little red and white cubes.

"Hey, Professor, where are the Pixelmon?!!" somebody yelled.

"YEAHHHH!!! WHERE ARE THE PIXELMON?!!! all the kids started yelling.

"Don't worry, they'll be out soon," the Professor said. But you could tell all the kids looked like they were about to tear the place apart unless they got to see the Pixelmon.

"All right, everybody, **COME OUT!**"

Suddenly, there was a flash of light and all the Pixelmon got zapped out of the cubes!

"WHOA!!!" all the kids yelled.

There were all kind of Pixelmon jumping around in the room. There were red ones, and blue ones, and yellow ones, and purple ones, big ones and small ones. . .it was awesome!

"YEAAHHHHHH!" the kids started yelling and screaming and losing all control.

"I WANT IT! IT'S MINE! I SAW IT FIRST!"

Next thing you know, all the kids started **GRABBING** and pulling at all the Pixelmon.

"SHHRRIIEEEK!!!"

"HHHIIISSSSSS!!!"

"SSNAAARRLLL!!!"

"SCCRREECCHH!!!"

Then, suddenly, the Pixelmon started attacking the kids.

The whole room went nuts.

Next thing you know, the Pixelmon started shooting fire out of their mouths and lasers out of their eyes!

**"EVERYBODY RUN!"** Ms. Bones yelled, right before a Pixelmon whipped its tail and clean knocked her head off. It must've flown into the other room because I could still hear her yelling from far away.

A Zombie Pigman kid tried to hide under a table until a huge dragon looking Pixelmon blew fire out of his mouth and burned the whole table.

It started to smell like the school cafeteria on a hot summer day. The

smell of rotten flesh
and bacon started
filling the air.

Me and the guys tried
hiding behind a **COUNTER**, but a
huge snake looking Pixelmon hovered
right above us and was about to chomp
down on us with its giant sharp teeth.

We all just grabbed each other and
closed our eyes, when suddenly. . .

"PIXELCHUUUUUUUU!!!"

ZZZZZAAAAAPPPP!!!!!

Pixelchu blasted a lightning bolt at the
snake and blew him half way across
the room.

That was enough to startle all the Pixelmon, and they stopped attacking for a moment.

"EVERYBODY GET OUT!!!" the Professor yelled.

Then all the kids ran out carrying Ms. Bones' **HEADLESS** body.

"Is everybody out?" Ms. Bones asked. . . or I think she asked since her headless body was just waving its arms all around.

"Has anyone seen Arnold the Creeper?"

Next thing you know, we heard a big **EXPLOSION** behind us.

I guess somebody forgot to tell Arnold we were leaving.

"YEAAAAHH!!! PIXELMON ARE AWESOME!!!" the kids started yelling and screaming.

All the kids would talk about on the way home was how many Pixelmon they were going to catch.

But I was just happy that I already had my Pixelmon.

I opened my bag, and Pixelchu was sleeping. I guess he was exhausted from all the **CRAZINESS.**

Pixelchu, I thought, you're my best friend.

Then I patted him on the head. . .

ZZZZAAAAAAPPP!!!!

# ☀ THURSDAY ☀

A lot of kids called in sick from school today.

The whole school was like a **GHOST TOWN.**

But I knew where they all went. . .

They all went to the Forest Biome to try to find Pixelmon.

Ms. Bones was out, too. The principal said it was for personal reasons.

But I knew she was probably out looking for Pixelmon too.

Anyway, the only kids who came to class were Skelee, Slimey, Creepy, Ichabod and me.

Which is great because I wanted to show Pixelchu to all the guys at lunch.

When **LUNCH** came, I sat at our table, but all the guys were sitting with Ichabod for some reason.

When I got closer, I heard them talking about Pixelmon.

"Well, my Pixelmon is called an Enderdragonite," Ichabod said. "That's a mini Ender dragon, you know."

"Whoa!" was all the guys could say as they wiped the drool off their chins.

"Hey, guys, I got a Pixelmon too!" I said. "I found it in the swamp."

"In the swamp? I thought you could only find Pixelmon in the Forest Biome?" Skelee asked.

"Yeah, and how did you catch it so quick?" Slimey asked.

"Well, I doubt someone like you could ever find a real Pixelmon," Ichabod said rolling his eyes. . .and sticking his little **PINKY BONE** up at me.

"I did so! And I'll show you. He's in my bag!"

Then I put my bag on the table, and I started to zip it open.

I couldn't wait to see the look on their faces when they see I have the best Pixelmon ever.

Especially Ichabod. I can't wait to see how dumb he's gonna look when he meets Pixelchu.

Well, it's probably going to be hard since skeletons don't have faces, but I know he's gonna feel real dumb. . .

**"THERE HE IS!"** I said proudly as I pulled out Pixelchu.

"AAAAAAAHHH!!!"

"WHAT IS THAT THING?!!!"

"GET IT AWAY BEFORE IT BITES ME!!!"

"ITS MOVING! RUN!!!"

That's the last thing I heard before all the guys just scattered.

## HISSSSSS!

"Don't worry Pixelchu," I said. "They don't know you like I do."

"Chu?"

"Yeah, we're friends. . .forever."

"CHUUUU!!!"

Yeah, Pixelchu really liked that. . .

ZZZZAAAAAAPPP!!!!

. . .a lot.

# FRIDAY

Today the school was full of kids again.

All the kids were back and they were carrying bookbags full of Pixelmon they had caught.

And at lunchtime all the kids were **SHOWING OFF** their new Pixelmon.

"I got a Snotlax!"

"I got a Creeperchu!"

"I got a Skelesaur!"

"I got a Squaddle!"

"I got an Endermite!"

"Hey, that's not a Pixelmon!"

"Yeah, I know. . .but they're soooooo cool."

I wanted to show off my Pixelchu, but they would probably laugh me out of the cafeteria like they did yesterday.

There's only so much **HUMILIATION** a thirteen-year-old Zombie can take in his life, you know.

"Hey, Zombie, did you bring your Pixel-rat to school today?" Ichabod said really loud.

"HAHAHAHAHAHA!!!" was all I heard as I quickly made my way to the janitor's closet.

I've gotten really used to the janitor's closet since I've been in middle school.

What can I say. . .it's my **HAPPY PLACE.**

All of a sudden, I started hearing a lot of commotion out in the schoolyard.

"Hey, it's Team Cube!"

I ran out to see what all the fuss was about. There was a big crowd outside circling these two mob kids.

"So you wanna battle, huh?" A tall Illager kid with a headband said.

If you don't know what an
**ILLAGER** is, they're like Villagers,
but like, really mean.

Think Minecraft Biker Gang. . .

They just recently moved to our
neighborhood from Steve's Village.

Steve said that they were causing a
lot of trouble there, so he and a bunch
of the other villagers kicked them out.

I think they're related to Zombie Villagers, but they're not green and beautiful like we are.

"Well, I'm ready!" the Illager kid said. "Bruh-Ninja, I choose you!"

Next thing you know, the Illager kid threw out his red and white cube and after a flash, a tall skinny Pixelmon with an afro jumped out."

## "BRUH-NINJA!"

"Oh, yeah?!" Then the other kid, threw out his cube and said, "PEE-YEW, I choose you!"

Then a round fluffy Pixelmon jumped out.

"PEE-YEW!"

"All right, let's **BATTLE!**" The Illager kid said. "Bruh-Ninja, use Bro-Kick!"

"Bruh-Ninja! Hyahhh!"

Then the tall Pixelmon with the afro kicked the little round Pixelmon halfway across the schoolyard.

"Ooooooh!" all the kids said.

Then the other kid got really mad. "Oh yeah? PEE-YEW, use REPEL!"

"PEE-YEW!. . .FFRRRRNNTTT!"

"Oh, man, that stinks!" the crowd yelled.

Next thing, the tall Pixelmon took a whiff and started hurling chunks of something he ate.

"Think you got me, huh?!!" The Illager kid said. "Bruh-Ninja use BACK SLAP!"

"BRUH-NINJA!"

Then Bruh-Ninja began to back slap the little round Pixelmon repeatedly.

"PEE-YEW! USE SILENT BUT **DEADLY!**"

Then the little round Pixelmon started staring off into space. Then after a few seconds. . .

"UUUURRRGGGHH!" the crowd yelled.

Bruh-Ninja yelled too as he dropped the little Pixelmon and pulled his afro over his face.

"Let's finish this!" Then the Illager kid yelled, "BRUH-NINJA, USE **FANG ATTACK!!!!**"

"BRUH-NINJAAAAAAHHHHH!!!!!"

SLAM!

All of a sudden, some huge fangs came out of the ground and snapped shut on the little Pixelmon.

"PEE-YEW!" the other kid yelled.

Then after the smoke cleared, PEE-YEW was just lying there unconscious.

And then a voice came out of nowhere and said, "And Pee-Yew is unable to battle! Bruh-Ninja wins!"

"That's what you get for **MESSING** with Team Cube!" the Illager kid said.

"Whoa!" the crowd responded.

Then he snapped his fingers, and a Slime wearing a headband joined him and they started walking away.

"Way to go, Johnny!" the Slime said as he tried to give the Illager kid a high-five.

Then, as they were walking away, suddenly an Ocelot with a headband got up on two feet, put his paw up in the air and made a motion like he dropped a mic.

Then they all strutted away with their headbands gleaming in the night.

"What was that?" I asked the guys.

"That was a Pixelmon battle!" they said. "Kids have been having them all day."

"That was. . .AWESOME!!!!" I said.

"Yeah, the principal even said that they were going to put on a big Pixelmon **TOURNAMENT** next week," Creepy said. "I think it was the only way to get the kids to stop destroying school property with their Pixelmon."

My mind was racing. All I could think about on my way home was about how

I was going to become the greatest Pixelmon trainer ever.

But that meant that I needed to win the tournament next week.

Then I looked in my bag at Pixelchu sleeping.

Don't worry, buddy, I'm gonna **WHIP** you into shape. They're never gonna laugh at us again because you're going to win the tournament and be the greatest Pixelmon ever!

# SATURDAY

Today, I decided to start **TRAINING** Pixelchu.

I didn't know where to start, so I decided to ask Steve for help.

"What is that?" Steve asked.

"It's my new Pixelmon. I found him in the swamp next to where my dad works at the Nuclear Waste Plant."

"Uh. . .Zombie, I don't think that's a Pixelmon. . .looks more like a naked mole rat," Steve said.

What does Steve know about Pixelmon? He's never had one, so he probably wouldn't know what they look like, anyway.

"Whatever, Steve. Anyway, I need you to help me train my Pixelmon because there's gonna be a Pixelmon tournament next week."

"Uh. . .Okay. . .whatever you say, man," Steve said.

"So we need to train Pixelchu to battle all types of Pixelmon, especially Johnny's," I said.

"JOHNNY! Are you messing with that Illager kid?" Steve asked. "Man, that kid is **TROUBLE.** He almost burned down half of my village because he wanted to see who would win a breakdance contest between a Creeper and a Magma Cube."

"Yeah, well, he's got the strongest Pixelmon I have ever seen named Bruh-Ninja. . .and I got to get Pixelchu ready to battle him."

"All right man. But watch out for that guy," Steve said. "You never know what kind of **DIRTY TRICK** he's gonna pull."

So, me and Steve started setting up an obstacle course for Pixelchu.

Steve started punching some trees and putting up blocks for Pixelchu to jump over.

I set up a few traps to get Pixelchu ready to face Bruh-Ninja's Fang attack.

"All right buddy, LET'S GO!"

But Pixelchu just laid down on the grass and went to **SLEEP**.

"Come on buddy. . .come on. . .you can do it. . .come on. . ."

Nuthin'.

Then I heard somebody laughing behind us.

"HAHAHAHA! What's the matter Zombie? Is your Pixel-rat unable to battle? HAHAHAHA!"

Oh, man, it was Ichabod.

Then Ichabod walked over to me and Steve with that smug look on his face. . .or, I'm sure he did.

"Steve, this is Ichabod. Ichabod this is Steve."

"Pleasure to meet you, Steven. I am Ichabod Percival Freely, from the **WOODLAND FREELY ROYAL FAMILY**, thirteenth generation on my mother's side. But my friends call me I.P."

"What's wrong with your pinky, man?" Steve asked.

"Well, I never!" Ichabod said as he stormed away. . .and rolled his eyes.

"Ooooh-key. That was weird," Steve said.

"Yeah, that guy is so spoiled, he makes rotten flesh taste like cotton candy," I said.

"Yeah, or that guy is **SO SPOILED** he gets dizzy playing on his high horse," Steve said.

"Or, that guy is so spoiled he took a selfie when the teacher told him to pay attention," I said.

"Or, that guy is so spoiled that when his mom makes bratwurst, she calls him for advice," Steve said.

Then, we just looked at each other and burst out laughing.

Then, we looked over at Pixelchu sleeping.

"So what are we going to do about training Pixelchu?"

"Come on, Pixelchu. I believe in you. You can do it," I whispered to little Pixelchu.

**NUTHIN'.**

"All right, Zombie. If it's a battle you want, it's a battle you'll get!"

We turned around and it was Ichabod looking really mad and holding a little red and white cube.

"Okay, Enderdragonite, I choose you!"

"RRROOARRR—ENDERDRAGONITE!"

Oh, man, what was I going to do? Pixelchu was just lying there like a lumpy potato.

"Okay, ENDY, USE SPIT WAD!"

"ENDERDRAGONITE! HHHAACCCKKK. . . PEWWWW!"

Then what looked like a **HUGE GLOB** of snot on fire came hurling at me, Steve and Pixelchu.

"Oh, man, Zombie. I think we're in trouble!" Steve said. "RUN!"

But it was too late. The giant fiery spit wad was about to slather us in red hot jello.

"PIXELCHUUUUUUU!!!"

ZZZZZAAAAAPPPP!!!!!

Suddenly, a giant lightning bolt came out of nowhere and cut through the snot ball and blasted Enderdragonite right out of his skin.

He landed on Ichabod knocking them both down.

Then, a voice came out of nowhere. "And Enderdragonite is unable to battle. Pixelchu **WINS!**"

Man, where is that voice coming from?

"YEEEAAHH!!! Zombie that was awesome!" Steve said. "How did he do that?"

"I don't know, he just does it."

"Well, it looks like Pixelchu only responds when he feels like he's being **ATTACKED.** So now we know how to get him going," Steve said.

So then we spent all day training Pixelchu.

We had to dress up like hostile mobs in order to get him moving.

But, Pixelchu was awesome. He never let up.

Blast after blast, he took **EVERYTHING** we threw at him.

I think Pixelchu is gonna beat every Pixelmon out there, even Bruh-Ninja.

Pixelmon tournament, here we come!

But I think me and Steve are gonna need a few days to grow our teeth back.

Ouch.

# ✳ SUNDAY ✳

"AAAAAAAHHH!!!"

I heard a loud **NOISE** that woke me out of bed.

"ZACKARY JULIUS ZOMBIE! YOU GET DOWN HERE RIGHT NOW!!!"

Oh, boy, what did I do now?

"Look at this!"

"Whoa."

The whole kitchen looked like a Creeper convention at a Cactus factory.

"Nice touch, Mom."

"That's not funny! The whole house is a mess, and it was all because of that RODENT I told you to get rid of!" my mom said.

Oh, man! Pixelchu must've snuck out of my room while I was sleeping!"

"Don't worry, Mom. I'll find him and get him out of the house now, I promise."

"Well, it's too late. I called the exterminator and they just left a few minutes ago with that. . .THING!"

"WWWWHHAAAATTTT!!!!"

All I could think about was all my hopes and dreams of becoming the greatest Pixelmon champion of the Minecraft World going down the drain.

"And you, young Zombie, are going to clean up this mess or you can kiss your Pixelmon tournament **GOODBYE!**"

Man, I'm going to miss the Pixelmon tournament and I'm going to miss my chance at become a Pixelmon Master!

But then it hit me. . .

"Uh, Mom. . .the Exterminator is going to find a nice home for Pixelchu, right?"

Silence filled the room.

Then I realized they weren't called Exterminators for nothing!

"Oh no! Pixelchu!"

I dropped everything and ran out of the house.

"ZACK, YOU COME BACK HERE RIGHT NOW OR BLAH, BLAH, BLAH, BLAH, FOR THE REST OF YOUR LIFE!" was all I heard in the background.

But I had to **SAVE** my buddy from getting exterminated. . .

I just had to!

# ☀ SUNDAY ☀
## LATER
## THAT DAY...

When I finally made it to the Exterminators, it was closed.

*That's weird, I thought. Then who were those guys that came to the house?*

And when I went around the back, there were these **SUSPICIOUS** looking Endermen selling cages full of Pixelmon to Team Cube!

Whoa. What's going on?

So, I snuck up a little closer to get a better look.

"Man, the boss is gonna be really happy when we bring him all these Pixelmon!" the Ocelot with the **HEADBAND** said.

"Yeah! He needs as many as he can get for his big experiment at Woodland Mansion," the Slime said.

"We still need more," Johnny the Illager said. "And I know exactly where to get them."

Then they all looked at each other with a creepy smile and said, "THE PIXELMON TOURNAMENT. . . HAHAHA!"

Then the Ocelot lifted his paw again and made a motion like he dropped the mic.

"You really need to stop that you know," Johnny said.

They were loading all the different CAGES of Pixelmon onto a truck.

But there were so many, I couldn't see Pixelchu.

"Eeeeewwww! Look at this one! I think it's sick!" the Slime said.

It was Pixelchu!

"Oh, man, I think I'm gonna hurl," the Ocelot blurted.

"Well, get rid of him! We can't bring that thing to the boss!" Johnny said.

"Man, why do I get stuck with the dirty jobs?"

So, the Ocelot with the headband let Pixelchu out of his cage, but Pixelchu just laid there.

"Move, you pink, stinky, flesh pile!" then the Ocelot started poking him with a stick.

## ALL OF A SUDDEN. . .

ZZZZAAAAAAPPP!!!!

Suddenly, all the Pixelmon's cages flew open.

Team Cube were so busy putting out the fire and trying to catch the Pixelmon that they didn't see me sneak up and pick up Pixelchu.

"Don't worry," I whispered. "I'm here, buddy."

"Chu. . .Chu," Pixelchu said as he gave me a **WRINKLY** smile.

So, I got back to my house, but I knew I couldn't keep Pixelchu there.

So, I went to see Steve.

"Wath up, Zombie?"

"Hey, Steve, how you feelin'?"

"Gooth, haws it goingth?"

"Good. . .so, did you find your missing teeth?"

"Naw, buth ith all right. I hath a feeling thath the tooth fairy isnth real. . .Whath up?"

"Hey, I wanted to see if I can keep Pixelchu with you for a while," I said. My mom is giving me a **REALLY HARD** time about him."

Even though Steve was a little weirded out by Pixelchu, he still let me keep him there.

I think he said something about how he was doing a new experiment and that Pixelchu could help him.

Something about creating a potion that brings mobs back from the dead.

Yeah, Steve can be weird sometimes.

Especially when he ends his sentences with a maniacal laugh.

"MUAHAHAHAHA!"

Well, at least I don't have to worry about my mom calling the Exterminators on Pixelchu anymore.

But what was Team Cube doing with all those Pixelmon?

And who was THE BOSS?

And where did they get all of those Pixelmon from?

After cleaning the mess at my house, and being grounded for the rest of my life, I was too tired to think about it.

All I wanted to do was to sleep for a week and wake up to battle at the Pixelmon tournament!

# M*NDAY

Everything was back to normal at school today.

The kids promised not to bring their Pixelmon to school since the principal promised to put on the Pixelmon tournament.

But some kids looked **REALLY SAD.** And some were even crying.

I guess the school cafeteria ban on mystery meat was finally lifted.

Although, I still think that stuff has some major side effects.

For some reason, after I started eating it, I started growing hair on my thumbs.

My skin started clearing up too.

. . .not cool for a zombie kid in middle school.

"What's up, guys? Hey, why are all those kids crying?"

"Some kids' Pixelmon have gone **MISSING,**" Skelee said.

"I think they just ran away because of their stance against animal cruelty," Slimey said.

"Or they could've spontaneously combusted," Creepy said.

We all just looked at Creepy for a minute.

"Hey, I saw **TEAM CUBE** yesterday and they had a bunch of Pixelmon in cages," I said. "I bet they had something to do with it."

"Whoa."

"What do you think they're doing with the Pixelmon?" Slimey asked.

"I don't know, but they were talking about a boss, and a big experiment that he was doing at a place called Woodland Mansion."

"Woodland Mansion!" We heard somebody yell behind us.

It was Ichabod. I swear, sometimes it feels like that guy is stalking me.

"What's Woodland Mansion?" Skelee asked.

"Woodland Mansion is a terrible place where some of the most ATROCIOUS experiments in history have been conducted. It has even been said that is where the recipe for mystery meat was first created."

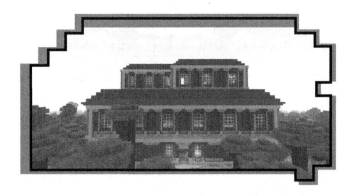

"Whoa."

"Except, Woodland Mansion was closed down because of **ILLEGAL** experimentation," Ichabod continued. "It hasn't been used in years, by the order of the high constable of Woodland. . .that's my uncle."

"So what's Team Cube doing there, and who is this boss character?" I said. "And what do they need all of those Pixelmon for?"

"Did someone mention our name?"

"Team Cube!"

Then the Ocelot jumped out and started his battle cry, "To protect the world from. . ."

"Don't say it," Johnny blurted.

"Aw, man," the Ocelot said.

"We heard you guys talking about us, and we thought someone was ready for a Pixelmon battle," Johnny said.

We all just looked at our feet. That's because even if we had our Pixelmon, nobody wanted to battle Bruh-Ninja and his deadly Fang Attack.

"That's what I thought," Johnny said. "Come on, boys. I'm tired of chicken, let's go get some **REAL FOOD.**"

Then as they were walking away, the Ocelot jumped out, lifted his paw and made a motion like he dropped a mic.

"You really don't know what that means, do you?" Johnny said as they walked away.

"So, Zombie, what's gonna happen to the missing Pixelmon?" Creepy asked.

"I don't know, but we have to do **SOMETHING.** Since it has something to do with Woodland Mansion, were going to have to go there."

When Ichabod heard that, he took out his Pixelmon cube and zapped himself into it.

"Something tells me Ichabod didn't like that idea," Skelee said.

Then we all gave each other a look that just said. . .Whoa.

#  TUESDAY

So, Professor Spruce let us visit his lab for our field trip again today.

I think the Professor felt bad about Ms. Bones getting her head knocked off by one of his Pixelmon.

When all the kids heard we were going to Professor Spruce's lab, they started getting so **EXCITED** that they started going crazy again.

But Ms. Bones said that if we ever embarrassed her again, she would make sure that we all missed the Pixelmon tournament.

Then all the kids got really quiet.

Yeah, Ms. Bones can be pretty tough.

But she hasn't been herself lately.

She almost cancelled our field trip at the last minute.

I think she said something about feeling a little **LIGHTHEADED**. ౦ ౦

Or was it something about leaking spinal fluid?

Whatever. I can't remember. All I care about is that today we're going to learn more about Pixelmon!

I wanted to bring Pixelchu with me to show Professor Spruce and all the other kids.

After meeting him, I was sure the Professor was going to say, "You are a really lucky Zombie, Zack. . .With Pixelchu at your side, you're going to be the **GREATEST** Pixelmon Master ever. . . Can I have your autograph?"

Yeah, I was going to show those kids who their real Pixelmon Daddy is.

But Steve said he needed Pixelchu's help with his experiment today.

Something about creating a potion that could turn wood into cake.

Like I said, Steve can be really weird sometimes.

When we got to the lab, they were still fixing things up after our last visit.

I couldn't tell if Professor Spruce was happy to see us or not.

But I could tell he was really happy to see Ms. Bones.

"Why, Ms. Bones, you've done something with your hair," Professor Spruce said.

"Do you like it? I just came from the **HAIRDRESSER,** tee, hee, hee. . ."

Oh, brother. More like the nose-hair hairdresser.

Everybody knows that Skeletons don't have hair.

. . .At least not on their heads.

This time, Professor Spruce talked about the power of Pixelmon.

Slimey kept trying to raise his hand while the Professor was talking, which probably made the Professor really mad.

"Yes, Slimey. What is it?"

"Professor. . .uh. . .what's the most **POWERFUL** Pixelmon ever?"

"Yeah, what is it?" the kids started yelling.

"I bet it's mine!"

"No way, it's mine!"

"Ahem! "Professor Spruce said, clearing the hole in his throat. "The most powerful Pixelmon ever documented was not really a Pixelmon at all. It was a genetically enhanced mutated specimen, grown in a lab. It was called, **EXPERIMENT 115.** It was created through illegal experimentation at the labs at Woodland Mansion."

"Whoa!" everybody said.

"This specimen was so powerful that when in a heightened state it could generate bolts of lightning that it could hurl through its nostrils," the Professor continued.

"Whoa!" everybody said again.

"What happened to it?" one of the kids asked.

"Well, after they closed the labs at Woodland Mansion, it was brought here for us to do research on it. We studied it for months until the **ACCIDENT.**"

"What accident?!!!" all the kids yelled.

"Yes, well, one of the researchers, who will remain nameless, uh. . . accidentally fed him some cake. . .Err, it wasn't his fault, you know. . .It's just that the little guy was so cute and. . ."

Then, all the kids started staring at Professor Spruce.

"Well, Experiment 115 wasn't used to the delicious combination of sweet flavors, and it went critical. . ."

"Huh!" the kids gasped.

"Yes, the explosion was so great it blew a hole right through the fabric of reality and disrupted the space time continuum."

"What the what?!!!" all the kids said together.

"Yes, it almost brought our species to **EXTINCTION.** Now, the government tried to cover it up by planting false news reports like that Mojang was acquired by Microsoft or that there was a major Minecraft Combat update. . .But the truth was that Experiment 115 had unleashed a force so destructive, it was almost the end of life on Minecraft World as we know it."

"So, what happened?!!!" all the kids blurted at the edge of their seats.

"Well, the Zombie Military decided that Experiment 115 was too **DANGEROUS** to live peacefully with society along with the fact that his very existence threatened all life in the universe. So, they decided to call the Exterminator."

"Huh!"

"Yes, we were all very sad when they called the **EXTERMINATOR,**" the Professor said as a tear fell from one of his eye sockets.

"Did the Exterminator, uh. . .exterminate him?!!" one of the kids asked.

"They never got the chance," the Professor said. "Someone in the lab, who will remain nameless to protect the innocent, err. . .released the cute little guy into the **SWAMP** behind the Nuclear Waste Plant. No one has seen Experiment 115 since."

"Whoa!"

"Professor, what were you doing when all this happened?" one of the kid's asked.

"Uh. . .I was in my office minding my own business. . .err, but I heard you are all going to participate in the Pixelmon tournament this weekend. He, he," the Professor said suspiciously.

"Yeah, it's going to be awesome," one kid said.

"My Snotlax is going to win," another kid said.

"No, way! My Spidernite is going to take it all!"

"Not if it battles my Squaddle, he's a water type so he has the **ADVANTAGE** over everybody!"

Next thing you know, the kids pulled out their Pixelmon cubes and started hurling them throughout the lab.

"Skelesaur, I choose you!"

"E-Feet, I choose you!"

"Char-lizard, I choose you!"

"Endermite, I choose you!"

"Hey, that's not a Pixelmon!"

"Yeah, but it's soooo cool!"

Then the whole lab went crazy.

Mrs. Bones was trying to keep her head, but all the screaming and yelling made it difficult to get **CONTROL.**

Suddenly, there was a flash of light and all of Professor Spruce's Pixelmon came out again.

SNARL!

SKREECH!

SHRIEK!

PFFFFTTT!

THWACK!

Yup. There goes Ms. Bones.

I guess she's gonna need to make another appointment at the head dresser.

"EVERYBODY OUT!!!!!" Professor Spruce yelled.

All the kids got **KICKED OUT** by Professor Spruce, again.

So, we all grabbed Mrs. Bones' body and ran out.

Except this time, we made sure to tell Evan, Arnold the Creeper's brother, we were leaving.

But right when we got outside. . .
BOOM!

Yeah, we forgot to tell Rory. . .his cousin.

On the way home, Creepy kept asking me questions about Pixelchu.

"Hey, Zombie, didn't you say you found Pixelchu in the swamp behind the Nuclear Waste Plant?"

"Hey, Zombie, didn't you say that Pixelchu can shoot lightning bolts?"

"Hey, Zombie, doesn't Pixelchu look like a genetically enhanced **MUTANT** that was the result of illegal experimentation? Creepy asked.

"Uh. . .Yeah. . ."

"Wow, wouldn't it be funny if Pixelchu was the genetic mutation that the Zombie Military was so afraid of that they want to get rid of it because it **THREATENED** all life on Minecraft World and existence as we know it?"

"He. . .he. . .That would be funny. . .He he. . ." I said.

"Wow, Pixelmon are so awesome," Creepy said. "I can't wait till I get one of my own."

"He he. . .yeah...great. . .one of your own. . .awesome. . .He he. . ."

Oh, man, something tells me I need to tell Steve.

# *TUESDAY*
## LATER
## THAT DAY...

I went to go see Steve, but there was a huge crater where his house used to be.

I heard some coughing coming from the rubble around the **GIANT CRATER.**

"Steve! What happened?"

"Cough, cough, well, I have successfully concluded that feeding Pixelchu gunpowder is not a good idea."

"What the what?!!! Why'd you do that?"

"Well, you know, Pixelchu is so cute, and little. . .and well he looked hungry, and. . ."

"I hope you didn't give him any cake!" I said.

"Why do you have some? I could use some of your mom's cake right now. I'm **STARVING.**"

"Speaking of Pixelchu," I said looking around, "where is he?"

"He's at the bottom of the crater," Steve said. "But watch out. He's still got a few good farts left in him."

We both climbed down into the crater.

And at the bottom, there was Pixelchu
sleeping like a baby.

All of a sudden, we heard, "PFFFT."

**"WATCH OUT!!!"** Steve yelled.

Then we both dove behind some rocks.

Then, after a few seconds. . .

"BOOOOOOOMMMM!!!!

"Yeah, there's a good three second
**DELAYED** reaction when his farts
combine with the Oxygen in the air."

Then, Pixelchu got up.

"Hey, buddy, how are you? I asked.

Pixelchu gave me a wrinkly smile.

"Who's a good boy? Who's a good boy?
Who's a good boy?" Steve kept saying
while licking his hands.

Something tells me Pixelchu didn't like
that.

ZZZZAAAAAAPPP!!!!

# WEDNESDAY

Ms. Bones missed school again today.

Actually, the Principal said that she was going to take the rest of the school year off.

Something about her head **MYSTERIOUSLY** going missing.

Yeah, something tells me that after yesterday, some of the kids made sure Ms. Bones wasn't going to be around to keep us from missing the Pixelmon tournament.

All the kids kept talking about all day was about the Pixelmon tournament.

They even snuck their Pixelmon into school to do **SECRET BATTLES.**

But, I figured they couldn't keep it secret for long.

Especially after they blew up the practice room for Creepers Glee Club.

I didn't bring Pixelchu to school today because I wasn't sure if he was dangerous or not.

I mean, could Pixelchu be Experiment 115 like Professor Spruce was talking about?

No way! Pixelchu is too nice. And he's so cute, he could never hurt a fly.

But, you know, I could test it by giving him a piece of my mom's cake.

Naw, that's **CRAZY!** I couldn't do that. I mean, what if he tears a whole in the universe?

Although, that would be really cool to see.

Then I ran into the guys at school.

"Wassup, Zombie? Hey, why are you looking so blue?" Skelee asked.

"Blue?!!! Seriously?!!! Oh, man, not that again!"

"Naw, man, that just an expression," Skelee said. "I mean, wassup?"

I decided to tell the guys the **TRUTH.**

"Well, guys, I'm not sure, but. . .I think Pixelchu is Experiment 115."

"No way!" Slimey said.

"That can't be," Skelee said.

"That's awesome," Creepy said.

"Brilliant!" Ichabod said. Though I don't know how he became one of the guys. . .especially using words like, 'Brilliant.'

So uncool.

"I was thinking of testing it out by giving Pixelchu some cake to see what would happen."

"Awesome!"

"Let's do it"

"I'm in!"

"**BRILLIANT!**"

"I mean, what's the worst that can happen, right?" I said.

"Yeah, and if anything does happen, we can just say that they came up with a new Minecraft Update," Skelee said.

"When are we going to do it?" the guys kept asking.

"Let's do it tomorrow, at my house. My mom said that she's baking a cake for the **PTA MEETING.** And she always makes extra for us."

"Awesome!"

"Can't wait!"

"Let's do it!"

"Brilliant"

Oh, brother.

After school, I went to see Steve so I could tell him about our experiment.

Then he put on a pair of glasses, a bowtie and started talking in a really weird voice.

"You see, Zombie, my thesis is that you must start with a basic hypothesis in order to properly apply the scientific method to this conundrum and properly attain a conclusion worthy of the annals of science."

Then he looked at me like he was constipated.

"PFFFFFTTTT!"

Then we both burst out **LAUGHING.**

"Hey can I come?" Steve said. "Plus, I can bring some of my equipment."

"I thought all we needed was cake."

"Yeah, and my equipment is my fork and knife, Ha ha!"

"PFFFFFTTTT!"

"All right, see you at my house tomorrow. And don't forget to bring Pixelchu."

"You got it!"

You know, I have a **NAGGING** feeling that I probably shouldn't do this experiment.

Like a really strong, nagging feeling.

A feeling right in the middle of my gut.

A feeling that. . .Oh, wait a minute. . .

Yank!

Oh! So that's where that grub went.

I thought it **GHOSTED** when I was eating lunch today.

Guess not.

Crunch!

So, what was I thinking about again?

Oh yeah. . .lunch.

# THURSDAY

After school today, all the guys and Ichabod came over to my house.

"Hey, what if we **BLOW** another hole in the fabric of reality and disrupt the space time continuum," Creepy asked.

"That would be so cool," Skelee said.

"Yeah, maybe I'll meet my clone in an alternate universe. . .I really hope he's cooler than me and has a girlfriend," Slimey said.

"I think your clone is a square no matter what universe he's from," Skelee said. "Ha, ha!"

"Zombie, do you think it's wise to fiddle with the **LAWS OF THE UNIVERSE?**" Ichabod said. "The consequences may be disastrous."

Yeah, I still don't know how this guy is part of the gang.

"Eh, what's the worst that can happen?" I said. "Plus, I think Professor Spruce was just saying all that stuff to impress Ms. Bones."

"Hey, did they find Ms. Bones head yet?" Creepy asked.

"Yeah, the Principal said she called and that she's coming back in a few weeks. He said something about Ms. Bones having a ball at the Soccer Championship in Mexico. . . or did he say she was the ball? Eh, I can't remember."

"Zombie! Your father and I are leaving for the PTA meeting," my mom yelled from downstairs.

So, me and the guys came downstairs to see them off.

"Zombie, please take care of your little brother while we're gone. . .and I left you and the boys some cake in the **REFRIGERATOR.**"

I wonder if I can do some experiments on my little brother? I thought. Muahahaha!

"Zombie, you know I can hear your right?" my mom said.

## WHAT THE WHAT?!!

"You really need to close your mouth when you think."

Then she gave me an embarrassing hug and kiss.

". . .And no experiments on your little brother."

"Okay, Mom. . ."

Then they left.

# "CAKE!"

"Woohoo!"

"Brilliant!"

We all dug into the cake until there was only one piece left.

"Hey, we need to save that piece for the experiment," I said. "So, make sure you don't eat it."

"Hey, Zombie. What's up with your booger collection?" Slimey asked. "I didn't see it in your room."

"Oh, yeah, it's gotten so big that I had to move it in the shed. Come check it out."

Then me and the guys all went to the shed.

When we got back to the house, Steve and Pixelchu were in the kitchen.

"Whuff up Zumbfie?" Steve said as he licked the ring of icing from around his mouth.

"Aw, man. That was our last piece of cake. What are we going to use for our experiment now?"

All the guys were really **BUMMED.** It's not every day you can rip a hole in the fabric of the universe.

"Hey, why don't we make our own cake?" Skelee said.

"Yeah, Zombie, I'm sure you've seen your mom make it like a thousand times, right?" Steve asked.

"Uh. . .yeah, I guess."

"Come on, ole chap. You can do it!" Ichabod said.

"Sure, why not."

"Brilliant!"

So, we all started tearing the kitchen apart looking for **INGREDIENTS** that looked like they belonged in a cake.

Then I got a big pot that we could throw stuff into.

"So, what'd you guys find?"

"Well, I found Wheat, Eggs, Milk, and Sugar," Creepy said.

"Great. Throw it in," I said.

"Hey, I found a **POTATO,**" Steve said. "But I've never seen a potato with green spots like these before."

"Eh. . .throw it in."

"I found a Beetroot," Slimey said.

"I found this," Skelee said, holding up a round purple fruit. "I think I saw a kid at school eating this once. . .and you know, now that I think of it, I haven't seen him at school since."

"Eh. . .throw it all in," I said.

"I found this," Ichabod said, holding up a jar of my nose hair collection.

"Throw it in," I said. "I like my cake with a little **EXTRA TEXTURE.**"

"How about these?" Skelee said, holding up a box of fireworks. "They could add some color to the mix."

"Uh. . .sure, throw it in."

We found a few more odds and ends in the kitchen and around the house and threw it into the pot.

We mixed it all together and poured into the biggest crafting table we could find and then. . .

"POP!"

Out popped a cake!

"Uh. . .is cake supposed to look like that?" Slimey asked.

"Eh, I'm sure it's fine. They say that some cakes come in ASSORTED flavors. . ." I said.

"What flavor is that?"

"From the looks of it, I'd say this one is probably Chocoslimebuttlivertoecheesee- arwaxpusfillednosehairbunionscab flavored," Steve said.

"Who wants to try it?" I said.

Then, we all turned to look at Ichabod. Perfect time for an **INITIATION.**

"Me? I'm sorry, gentlemen, but I am severely allergic," Ichabod said.

"Allergic to what?"

"Allergic to stupid," Ichabod said.

"Anybody else?"

Then we all looked at Creepy.

Naah, Zombie. I thought to myself.
Don't even think about it.

Well, nobody had the guts to try it.

"I guess I'll do it!" I said. Even though
I don't have guts.

"ZOMBIE! ZOMBIE! ZOMBIE! ZOMBIE!"
they started chanting my name.

So, I stuck my hand into our
**CREATION** and pulled out a chunk.

"ZOMBIE! ZOMBIE! ZOMBIE!
ZOMBIE!" they kept chanting.

Then I brought it closer to my face.

"ZOMBIE! ZOMBIE! ZOMBIE!
ZOMBIE!" Then they started getting
louder and louder.

Until finally. . .

GULP!

CHEW, CHEW, CHEW.

"Hey, Steve, I think he likes it!" Skelee said.

"I got to admit. . ." **CHEW**. . . **CHEW**. . . " It isn't that bad. Kinda tastes like a rubber tire, but with a nice tang to it. . .with a hint of mint. . .Almost like moldy pumpkin pie, but with a gamy flavor. . ." Chew. . .Chew.

"Great, so now we can test it on Pixelchu," Steve said.

So, Steve brought Pixelchu into the kitchen.

"Who's a good boy? Who's a good boy? Who's a good boy?" Steve kept saying.

ZZZZAAAPPPP!!!!!

After we put the fire out, we put a plate of cake in front of Pixelchu.

He started sniffing around the plate a little bit.

"Hey, I think he's gonna eat it," Skelee said.

Then the **RUMBLING** started.

"Uh. . .guys. . .I'm not feeling so good," I said.

"What's the matter, Zombie?"

"RRRRRUUUMMMBBBLLLEEEE!"

"What was that?" Steve asked.

"I think it was me," I said.

"You need to go number two?" Steve asked.

"More like two. . . **HUNDRED,**" I said.

Then the weirdest feeling came over me. It kind of felt like somebody took the lower half of my body and pulled it out of my nostrils.

Then one end of my body erupted. . .

"PFFPRTRTRGURTRUFNASUTUTUTP-RRTGGGGPHHLLGGGSPLLAATTT!!!!!"

"Oh, man! Run for cover," Steve yelled. "There's a three second delay!"

Then, Steve picked up Pixelchu and ran out of the kitchen.

Right when we made it out of the house we heard. . .

"BOOOOOOOMMMM!!!!"

# FRIDAY

Well, I stayed home from school again today.

Still recovering from the explosion.

Now you're probably wondering what **HAPPENED.**

Let's just say that the only hole in the universe that we ripped open was the one that's left where our kitchen used to be. . .

. . .And where my butt used to be.

Explosive diarrhea. . .

So wrong.

Yeah, I'm also **GROUNDED** again.

Not because I have no butt. . .

. . .But because of the explosion.

You, know. . .the one that gave me no butt.

Well, anyway. Now, I got no TV, no video games, no hang outs, no Internet and no cake. . .

For how long?

I don't know. . .my mom said something about BLAH, BLAH, BLAH, BLAH when the Nether freezes over.

We never did find out if Pixelchu is Experiment 115.

But it doesn't matter now. The Pixelmon tournament is tomorrow, and I'm gonna **MISS** it.

Man, I'm gonna miss all those cool Pixelmon battling each other.

I'm gonna miss all those cool Pixelmon moves.

And I'm gonna miss seeing who becomes the greatest Pixelmon trainer in all of Minecraft.

It was supposed to be me, but now. . . forget it!

All the guys are gonna to be there, the whole school is gonna be there, and even Steve is gonna be there.

And I'm gonna miss the whole thing.

## IT'S SO UNFAIR!

No way! I've got to figure out a way to get there.

No matter what it takes, I'm going to become the greatest Pixelmon trainer in all of Minecraft!

Rrruuuummmmbbblllleeee. . .

That is, if I make it through the diarrhea apocalypse. . .

. . .Oooooohhhhh.

# SATURDAY

I almost didn't make it to the tournament this morning.

My parents wanted to take me **SOMEWHERE SPECIAL** today because they wanted to cheer me up for losing my butt.

But I needed to make it to the tournament.

So, I made believe like I was still sick.

It was a little hard because Zombie butts grow back real fast.

So, I cut a hole in my bed and put my new butt in it.

Then I took a black marker and went to town on my face and arms.

I looked like an Enderman that lost a fight with a blender.

But, it worked like a **CHARM.**

My mom and dad decided to go out with my little brother instead and leave me home alone.

Whoever said that education is wasted on the young?

But, man, it's been an awesome tournament so far.

The kids brought some amazing Pixelmon to the tournament.

And the Pixelmon moves they did were amazing, too.

They had Pixelmon doing **STUFF** I had never seen before.

They had moves like:

- Air Biscuit
- Nose Picker
- Break Wind
- Toe Jam
- Back Wash
- Ugly Stick
- Wet Willie
- Dragon Breath
- Barking Spider

- ☒ John Cena
- ☒ Projectile Vomit

And one Pixelmon called a Creeperchu even had a move called Hydrogen Bomb.

He used it once in a battle, and it was awesome!

Except. . .he didn't make it to the finals.

But no matter how powerful the moves were, nobody could beat Bruh-Ninja's Fang Attack.

And now it was up to me because me and Pixelchu made it to the **FINALS**, too.

So, it was me and Pixelchu versus Johnny and Bruh-Ninja.

The battle is going to be tough especially since Pixelchu hurt his knee in the last battle.

The funny thing is, so did I.

It's like me and Pixelchu are bonded on a mental, emotional and physical level.

Even when we need to pee.

I'm just glad I'm wearing my dark pants.

Well, the finals are going to start in a few minutes.

But I thought I would jot down my thoughts, for history's sake.

You know, so they can teach Minecraft Mob kids about the GREATEST Pixelmon Players that ever lived.

Yeah, I know. I'm being modest.

Well, anyway, here we go!

# SATURDAY AFTERNOON

I can't believe it!

It was the most amazing battle ever!

The way Pixelchu fought was **GLORIOUS!**

I knew he could do it!

I'm just mad I'm not the Pixelmon champion of the world.

Yeah, just when you think a Zombie can finally get some respect around here, something always happens.

Now, you're probably wondering what happened. . .

Well, me and Pixelchu had Bruh-Ninja on the ropes. But, man, was he **STRONG.**

No matter how many lightning bolts Pixelchu shot at Bruh-Ninja, he took them all.

And he was still standing!

Pixelchu and I were still beat up from Bruh-Ninja's Back Slap attack. But we weren't gonna give up.

And Bruh-Ninja hadn't used his Fang Attack yet, but we knew it was coming.

"What do you think Pixelchu? Do you think you still have it in you to take it to the end?"

"Chu. . .Chu!"

"All right, buddy! Let's try something different. Pixelchu use **HEAD BUTT!**"

Pixelchu ran as fast as he could at Bruh-Ninja.

"BRUH-NINJA USE FANG!" Johnny yelled.

"BRUH-NINJAAAAAAHHHHH!!!!!"

SLAM!

Just as Pixelchu was about to land the winning shot on Bruh-Ninja, suddenly these large teeth came out of the ground and slapped shut on little Pixelchu.

"OH NO! PIXELCHU!"

Little Pixelchu was trapped in Bruh-Ninja's Fang attack.

I could tell that the Fang Attack was **DRAINING** Pixelchu of all his energy. It was draining my energy, too. And I kept getting weaker and weaker. But I couldn't do anything to stop it.

*I'm sorry, Pixelchu. We're gonna lose because I wasn't strong enough to help you. Forgive me, my friend.*

As Pixelchu and I were down on one knee, suddenly, I saw something glimmering from the corner of my eye socket.

It looked like a white and brown block with little red dots on it.

It flew across the sky toward Pixelchu in what looked like **SLOW MOTION.**

Until, finally, little Pixelchu used all his strength to jump up and catch it with his two front teeth.

IT WAS CAKE!

Somebody threw a piece of cake at Pixelchu.

Pixelchu devoured it quickly.

Suddenly, there was a rumbling sound and a giant white flash of light that came from where Pixelchu was standing and covered everything.

My whole thirteen-year-old life flashed before my eyes. Yeah, it went **PRETTY FAST.**

But the thing I thought of most was my friendship with Pixelchu.

*Pixelchu, even though we didn't win, I'm just glad that I met you and that you became my friend. I will never forget you.*

*Goodbye. . .*

Yeah. . .no.

The giant flash of light didn't kill us.

It just opened a giant portal where a giant robot came out that used a humongous vacuum cleaner to suck up all the Pixelmon up and transport them to another **DIMENSION.**

No, I'm serious.

There's like no Pixelmon left in Minecraft.

Even Pixelchu is gone.

Now everything is back to boring old Minecraft World.

And I'm back to my boring old middle school Zombie life.

What do you mean what am I going to do about it?

I have no idea. I'm just a thirteen-year-old Zombie. What am I supposed to do?

What do you mean that Pixelchu was my friend?

I know he was my friend.

I'm just. . .you know. . .**LAZY.**

What do you mean he needs my help?

How do you know, anyway?

You're just an annoying voice in my head that I am talking to while I'm writing in my diary.

Yeah. . .yeah. . .I know. . .it's not right, and I need to gather up the guys and do something crazy to save Pixelchu and all the Pixelmon, and save Minecraft World from utter **DEVASTATION** at the hands of a maniacal villain that is trying to take over the universe. Blah, blah, blah. . .

But where do I start? I don't even know where they are.

What do you mean Woodland Mansion is a great place to start?

Just because they did illegal experiments there, and it's where they first created Pixelchu, and Team Cube was talking about the boss and how the boss needs Pixelmon for a

big experiment, and that he's doing
his experiment at Woodland Mansion,
doesn't mean. . .

Uh. . .oh. . .yeah. . .

Okay. **YOU GOT ME.**

Let's do this.

# ☀ SUNDAY ☀

So, I gathered all the guys at my house.

"Hey, where's Steve?" I asked.

"He said he needed to grab some equipment," Skelee said. "He's coming over in a little bit."

"Well, guys, we need to **ATTACK** Woodland Mansion and rescue Pixelchu and all of the rest of the Pixelmon. Now who's with me?!!!"

All the guys just looked down at their feet like they were being asked to go out and sell Girl Scout cookies or something.

"What's the matter, guys? Where's your **FIGHTING SPIRIT?**"

"Zombie, it's just that. . .my uncle has told me scary things about Woodland Mansion," Ichabod said. "Where I am from, they even used to tell scary stories about Woodland Mansion to scare young children into eating their vegetables. And I've eaten a lot of vegetables."

"How about you, Creepy?"

"Zombie, Pixelmon are really cute and all, but I don't want to be used as somebody's experiment," Creepy said. "My uncle told me that in the old days, the government used to do experiment on Creepers. He even said that they found one of the Creeper Experiment Black Sites and they found Creeper entrails all over the walls. . .all over the walls, man!"

You know, that would explain a lot about Creepers. I don't think **EXPLODING** farts is something they picked up by accident.

"Yeah, Zombie," Skelee said. "And even if we find the Pixelmon, what are we supposed to do against that giant robot? You saw that thing. It was at least one hundred feet tall."

So, we were all just sitting there with a look of defeat on our faces when my mom and dad walked in.

"Boys, we heard what you were thinking of doing," Mom said. "And though everything inside of me is telling me it's too **DANGEROUS** and wants me to keep you home, we need to tell you a story. . ."

Then my mom and dad started telling us how when they were young they worked as lab assistants, along with an Illager named Guy and a young professor named Seymour Spruce. . .and a janitor named Old Man Jenkins.

"One day, we were all asked to help with a special government project at a lab secretly located at a place called. . .Woodland Mansion."

"Wha. . .!"

"In those days, there were Pixelmon everywhere in Minecraft World. Every boy and girl had a Pixelmon to call their own. And it was beautiful.

Then, suddenly, Pixelmon started **DISAPPEARING** and nobody knew why. Until, finally, they weren't any Pixelmon left.

Your father, Seymour and I worked with Pixelmon, you see, and so we tried to find out why they were disappearing.

Then one day, Old Man Jenkins told us that Guy was spending a lot of time on the third-floor of the Mansion at all hours of the night. So, we all decided to go to the third-floor to find out why Guy was spending so much time there.

Later, we discovered the real reason the Pixelmon were disappearing. Guy was STEALING all the Pixelmon and doing illegal experiments on them. He was trying to take all the Pixelmon's powers and absorb them for himself so that he could take over the Minecraft World.

Your father, Seymour, me and Old Man Jenkins tried to stop him, but it was too late. Guy had lost his mind, drunk with the desire for power. From then on, he called himself. . .The Evoker!"

"Whoa!"

"He had three minions under his **HYPNOTIC POWER** that used their Pixelmon to capture us and put us in prison cells. There was nothing we could do to stop him.

Except, by chance, a mouse snuck into the Evoker's machine and turned it on by accident.

Then, the mouse absorbed so much power from the Pixelmon that it mutated into a hideous creature and broke loose. The mutated specimen started to tear up the lab, and before the Evoker could get control of it there was a massive explosion that blew up the entire third floor of the mansion where the lab was.

By then, the Zombie military had stormed the Mansion and released us. They spent days trying to CAPTURE the hideous beast because it continued absorbing power. They even said it mutated into a different species. They finally captured the hideous beast and shut down the lab for good."

"What happened to the Evoker?" we asked.

"No one knows. But rumor has it that he secretly rebuilt the third-floor lab at Woodland Mansion. The rumors also say that he is desperately searching for the mouse that took the powers that should have belonged to him. He wants his powers back so he can take over Minecraft World as we know it."

"The Boss!" me and the guys yelled.

"So, guys, what's it going to be? Are we going to let the Evoker win and take over the Minecraft World? Or are we going to FIGHT for what is ours? WHO'S WITH ME?!!!!"

Then Ichabod pulled out his Pixelmon cube and zapped himself inside it again.

Oh, brother.

# ✳ SUNDAY ✳
## LATER
## THAT DAY

I finally convinced the guys to come with me.

But it took a lot of long speeches, a few Minecraft trading cards and a promise that my mom would make a cake for us, to finally get them going.

Then Steve made it just in time as my mom pulled the cake out of the crafting table.

It's like Steve has a **SIXTH SENSE** whenever there's cake around.

The good thing is that we're not alone on our quest.

Mom and Dad decided to come.

Yeah, I know. It's lame to have your parents come on a quest.

But they did represent with some serious **BATTLE EQUIPMENT.**

Actually, I think they just put on my dad's old Punk Rock Band stuff.

Either that or there was a sale on 1980's Post-apocalyptic cosplay.

Anyway, Mom and Dad knew the layout of the Woodland Mansion really well.

So, if we wanted to survive, we needed them to come with us.

When we got to the Woodland Mansion, it didn't look like it was closed anymore.

There were lights in some of the rooms and strange **BUZZING** and flashing lights coming from the top floor.

But, I've got to admit, the Woodland Mansion was huge. . .and scary.

There were so many rooms, I knew we were going to get lost in there. . . or worse.

"Be careful where you step," my dad said. "Every step you take can be your last. There are **LETHAL TRAPS** everywhere."

What the what!

"Just kidding. . .unless the Evoker knows were coming."

"Dad!"

When we all walked into the Mansion there was a huge passageway going to the right and another to the left.

"Where should we start looking?" Steve asked.

"The West Wing," my mom said with a serious tone. "Well, at least that's where the bathroom is and I've got to go. Zombies weren't meant to wear leather pants."

As soon as we started walking, the floors started creaking and suddenly we started hearing moaning and grunting **NOISES.**

I was starting to get really scared.

And it didn't help that Creepy kept hissing behind us.

"What's with the red carpet?" Skelee asked, pointing to the huge red carpet that covered the hallway floor.

"Probably to soak up all the **BLOOD,**" Steve said.

HSSSSSSS.

"Maybe we should split up?" Steve said.

"Seriously?!!! Haven't you watched any horror movies?"

"Yeah, but we'll cover more ground that way."

"That's actually a good idea," my mom said. "Francis, I'll take Zombie, Steve and his friend with the pinky and we'll go to the West Wing. You can take the other boys and go to the East Wing."

I think my mom really needed to use the bathroom.

"Sounds good, Mildred," my dad said. "C'mon, boys, I'll show you the indoor Boxing Gym where Mrs. Zombie and I used to practice **KARATAY!**"

Oh, yeah. . .bringing parents on a quest is lame.

Me, Steve and Ichabod left my mom in the bathroom, and we started exploring some of the rooms in the West Wing.

They had some **WEIRD STUFF** in there. They had a room with an altar to a plant, a room with a mountain of obsidian, and they even had a room with a giant Chicken.

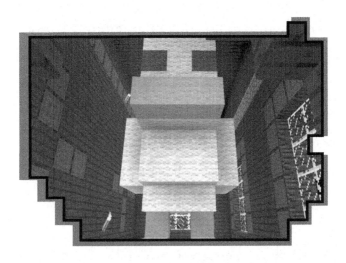

Like I said, weird.

My mom was taking a really long time. I think she wasn't kidding about those leather pants.

"Hey, let's go upstairs," Steve said.

"What about my mom?" I said.

"She seems like she can take care of herself," Steve said. "Did you see her Mohawk?"

"Uh, Okay," I said.

Ichabod, didn't say much. . .he was just **HYPERVENTILATING** into a paper bag most of the time.

So, Steve, Ichabod, and I decided to go upstairs to the second floor.

It was really dark there, so we started lighting torches.

Then out of the corner of my eye socket, I saw a strange figure at the end of the hall looking at me with these beady red eyes.

I couldn't see if it was Dad or one of the guys.

"Steve, light up a **TORCH**, will ya," I said.

As soon as Steve lit up the torch, I could see who it was.

It was Johnny, the Illager. Except this time, he wasn't carrying a Pixelmon ball. He was carrying a huge, scary ax in his hand.

"Uh, Johnny, you okay?" I asked him.
"What's with that big, scary looking. . .
um. . .really sharp ax you got there?"

Then, all of a sudden, Johnny started
walking slowly toward us. Then
he started walking faster. Then
he started running at us **FULL
SPEED,** waving that big ax over his
head and screaming at the top of his
lungs.

"AAAAAAAHHH!!!!" we yelled.

We all didn't want to stick around to find out what Johnny's problem was, so we ran into a really dark room and locked the door.

THWACK! THWACK! THWACK!

Johnny was hacking at the door trying to get in.

"I can't see anything," I whispered.

"Me, either," Steve whispered back. "Why are we WHISPERING?"

"Oh, yeah. . .sorry. Hey, light up a torch; it's really creepy in here."

As soon as Steve lit up the torch, we heard. . .

HSSSSSS.

Except it wasn't Creepy.

"AAAAAAAHHH!!!!"

BOOOOOMMM!!!!

Then the whole floor caved in below us
and we fell through.

**"AAAAAAAHHH!!!!"**

Next thing I know, I was hanging
on Steve, and Steve was hanging
on Ichabod, who just happened to be
hanging onto a wood block with his
pinky.

Oh, man, I never thought I'd be this
happy over a dude's pinky.

But my joy didn't last very long.

"Guys, I don't know how long I can hold this," Ichabod said as he slowly started to lose his pinky grip.

Next thing you know. . .

"AAAAAAAHHH!!!!"

As we were falling to our doom, all I could see was darkness all the way down, like if we were falling through the never-ending **ABYSS** for lost Minecraft characters.

"AAAAAAAHHH!!!!"

Squish!

What the what?

We landed on something weird and squishy.

Steve lit up a torch, and we found ourselves in a room full of cobwebs.

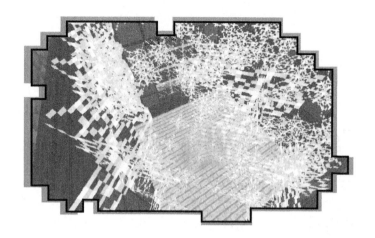

"YEEAAAHHHH!!!!" We all yelled, just glad that we were **STILL ALIVE.**

But then we heard. . .

TSK! TSK! TSK! TSK!

"AWWWWW!!!" we all yelled.

When we all turned around, there was a scary looking, drooling spider behind us.

Oh, man, this is it. I'm going to be Spider chow. . .

"**NATE!**" Steve yelled. "What are you doing here, buddy?"

What the what?!

TSK! TSK! TSK! TSK!

"What?" Steve said, like if he understood what the scary, drooling spider was saying. "You and the other Street Kids were kidnapped and brought to Woodland Mansion?"

TSK! TSK! TSK! TSK!

"And you were all forced to work as slaves to do the bidding of the **EVIL EVOKER?**"

TSK! TSK! TSK! TSK!

"And you tried to escape, but you were caught and they locked you in this room and threw away the key?"

TSK! TSK! TSK! TSK!

"And by blowing a hole in the ceiling we helped you escape?"

TSK! TSK! TSK! TSK!

"And now you want us to help you help all of the other Street Kids to **ESCAPE** the evil clutches of the Evil Evoker?"

"Come here, buddy," Steve said and gave the scary, drooling spider a hug and kiss.

Nasty.

"Dude, you understood all that?" I asked Steve.

"Naw, but I kinda figured that's what happened," Steve said.

After we **CLIMBED** through the roof of the cob web room, it seems that Johnny had given up trying to break down the door of the room upstairs.

So, we snuck out of the room and started heading back to find Mom and the others.

All of a sudden, we saw Creepy running hysterically, hissing all the way toward us.

"Zombie, it was terrible!" Creepy said. "They captured everybody! And they took everybody to the third floor! And they're going to do experiments on them! I know it!"

HSSSSSSS

"Oh, gosh!" Creepy said **HYSTERICALLY.** "Their entrails are going to be all over the waaaaalllsss!!!"

"Calm down, Creepy," I said, "or we'll all end up all over the walls."

After Creepy took a **MASSIVE PUFF** from his Liquid Nitrogen inhaler, he told us what happened.

"What are we going to do?" I asked Steve.

"Well, we need to split up," Steve said.

"Seriously?!!! What is with you and splitting up?"

"Me and Ichabod can help the Street Kids escape, and you and Creepy can go upstairs and help rescue your folks and everybody else," Steve said. "After we get the kids we'll come up and help you out."

I got to admit, it sounded like a **GOOD PLAN.** But I didn't like it.

I thought Ichabod would be a useless mess by now, but after seeing Steve with Nate, he found his courage.

"Don't worry, Zombie," Ichabod said. "We'll rescue those kids and come back for you."

Then, out of nowhere Ichabod **JUMPED** on Nate like he was born to ride a scary, drooling Spider.

"I wasn't named three-time Spider Jockey Woodland Race Champion for nothing!" he said.

"Jump on, Steve!" Then Ichabod yelled, "HEEYAH!"

Then, Ichabod, Nate and Steve galloped off into the sunset...

...Well, more like down the dark and creepy hallway.

But, wow. Who'd ever think that I.P. Freely could be **SO COOL**. ° °

# M�NDAY

Yeah, it's Monday already.

By now, you'd think I would be weirded out by the fact that daylight only lasts ten minutes in Minecraft.

But, I guess I'm used to it.

So, after Steve, Ichabod and Nate **GALLOPED OFF** to save the Street kids, me and Creepy started walking upstairs to the third floor of the Mansion.

HSSSSSSS

"Don't worry, Creepy," I said. "We'll be okay. You know how it usually goes. We go on some zany Minecraft adventure and then just when it looks like everything is going to go really bad, then I come up with some great idea and save the day."

"What if you were just **LUCKY?**" Creepy asked.

You know, he had a point. What if I was just lucky and this time my luck ran out?

After that, I started hissing too.


When we got up to the third floor, there was another long hallway leading to a room at the end.

I think both of us were really scared because we just kept finding **EXCUSES** to search the different rooms.

"Dude, look at this cool bedroom. . ."

"Dude, look at this cool food court. . ."

"Dude, look at this cool library. . ."

"Dude, look at this cool picture. . ."

Eventually, there was only one room left to search.

It was the room at the end, with the flashing lights coming from under the door. And a big, **FAT SIGN** on the front that said, 'LAB.'

"They're doing experiments on them in there!" Creepy said. "Oh, the horror!!!"

I got to admit, I was really scared too.

What if the Evoker turns my parents into like, **HUMAN PARENTS** or something?

I mean, I'm used to Steve, but I heard human parents are like the worst.

They try to make you eat vegetables, clean your room, clean the dishes, take a bath, or worst, they may even try to homeschool me!

I was terrified just thinking about it.

When we finally got to the door, Creepy and I looked at each other.

"Gulp. Here it goes," I said, grabbing the big handle to the killer lab.

Suddenly, a swarm of what looked like little Withers with  **BAT WINGS** started attacking us!

"AAAAAHHHHH!!!!"

We started running, but they were too fast and they kept poking us with their little swords.

"Owww! Oooch! Ouch!" Man, those things hurt.

But then I realized that getting **POKED** by these things was probably not going to end well for Creepy.

So, we ran into one of the nearby bedrooms.

Which didn't help because those little demons flew right through the walls.

I found a big bed sheet and I took off one of the beds, and I covered Creepy with it.

Then we ran into the library and grabbed as many books as we could find.

We started **THROWING** books at the little flying minions, which stunned them a bit, but not for long.

So, we decided to run as fast as we could, head first, into the deadly laboratory.

My mom did say I could be a **KNUCKLE HEAD** sometimes. Maybe now I can put it to good use!

"HHHEEEYYYYYAAAAAHHHHH!!!!"

# M✷NDAY
## LATER
## THAT DAY...

Well, we broke through the door and what we found was crazy!

No, there weren't entrails on the walls.

But it was just **AS BAD.**

Mom, Dad, the guys, all the Pixelmon, as well as Steve, I.P., Nate and the Street kids were all locked in tubes that were connected to a giant machine.

They all looked sickly, like if all of their life energy was being drained from their bodies.

Then I saw giant wires that led from the machine to two pods.

In one of the pods was Pixelchu, but he looked really sick too.

And the other pod was empty.

Suddenly, we heard the **SCARIEST** voice ever. . .

"WHO DARES ENTER MY LAIR?"

Cough, cough, Haaaaccckkk. Spit.

"I mean, can't a guy go to the bathroom without getting interrupted every few minutes?"

What the what?!

It was the Evoker. But he looked
like some dude in a robe. . .with a
**MAGAZINE** in his hand.

"Let go of my parents and my friends!"
I yelled, knowing it wasn't going to do
anything. But I thought I would try to
act tough anyway.

HSSSSSSS.

"Yeah, Creepy, not helping. . ."

"So, you're Francis and Mildred's kid?" the Evoker said. "I could see the resemblance. Especially since you're really good at interrupting."

"Well. . .Guy! What kind of name is Guy, anyway? Sounds like your mom and dad didn't really put a lot of **THOUGHT** into that one."

I could tell he didn't like that. But I needed to distract him long enough for Creepy to free Pixelchu and the others.

"Seriously. Could your name be any lazier? Like is your dog named 'dog' too?"

I think it was working because he was getting really, really mad.

"I mean, why couldn't your parents name you Dude, or Bro. . .which would've been much cooler by the way. . . But Guy? So lame. And another thing. . ."

"I'll FIX YOU! BRUH -NINJA I CHOOSE YOU!"

ZAP!

## BRUH -NINJA!

What the what?

"Surprised? Who do you think taught Johnny everything he knows?"

Great, I have to fight a Pixelmon battle, and I don't even have a Pixelmon!

"BRUH -NINJA, USE BACK SLAP!" the Evoker yelled.

Then suddenly, Bruh-Ninja jumped on top of me and started smacking me with a barrage of **BACK SLAPS.**

SLAPAPAPAPAPAPAPAPAPAP!

Oh, man, that hurt.

"And I also have a few tricks you haven't seen!" the Evoker said. "BRUH-NINJA, USE BEAT DOWN!"

Then Bruh-Ninja launched an onslaught of punches in my direction.

POW, POW, POW, POW, POW, POW, POW!

Man, this hurts. I think this is it. I don't think I'm gonna make it.

"All right Bruh-Ninja, finish him with MEGA FANG ATTACK!"

Mega-Fang Attack?!!! What in the world is that?

Suddenly, not one, but like a hundred fangs came out of the ground and came toward my direction ready to **SNAP** my body like a twig.

Oh, man. I'm a goner for sure, I thought as I closed my eyes.

Goodbye, cruel world. . .

"PIXELCHUUUUUUU!!!"

ZZZZZAAAAAPPPP!!!!!

Suddenly, the biggest **LIGHTNING BOLT** I had ever seen came flying through the air and blasted Bruh-Ninja and the Evoker right out of the window of the Mansion.

KKRRESSHHHH!

Then Pixelchu collapsed after that last energy blast.

"PIXELCHU!"

I ran over to little Pixelchu, who looked hurt.

"Creepy, quick, get my parents and the other kids out."

Pixelchu used his last bit of energy to save me. I could see the **LIFE DRAINING** from his wrinkly little body as a tear came down one of his eyes.

"Oh, Pixelchu, you can't die! You're my friend. You and me we're going to be the greatest Pixelmon team ever! And we are going to win the Pixelmon championship, and. . .Pixelchu?"

"Chu. . .Chu. . . chu. . ."

And he was gone.

Suddenly, the entire Mansion began to shake.

"THIS MANSION WILL SELF DESTRUCT IN THIRTY SECONDS," a voice said out of nowhere.

Oh, man, the entire place was going down. But everybody was too drained of energy to run out of here.

"TWENTY-FIVE, TWENTY-FOUR, TWENTY-THREE. . ."

Only **SOLUTION** was to go out the broken window.

"EVERYBODY! WE NEED TO JUMP!"

They all agreed, even though we all knew we would be seriously hurt from a fall from the top of Woodland

Mansion. And some of us were so weak, we knew we might not make it. But it was better than being blown to bits.

I grabbed Pixelchu's **LIFELESS BODY**, and I helped the others to the ledge of the broken window.

"EIGHTEEN, SEVENTEEN, SIXTEEN. . ."

"GRAB THE TOTEM OF UNDYING!" I heard somebody say.

What the what?!!

It was Johnny and Team Cube!

Oh, man! Not these guys again.

"GRAB THE TOTEM OF UNDYING!" Johnny kept saying as he pointed to a

small, gold looking idol with green eyes
that was on the floor.

I thought it was a trick, but Johnny
didn't have his **RED EYES** or his
huge, sharp scary ax,
thank goodness.
Plus, he and the
rest of Team cube
were helping
everybody get to the
ledge.

So, I picked up the totem in one hand
and carried Pixelchu in the other hand.
Then, I joined everybody on the ledge,
as we all linked arms. . .

"SIX, FIVE, FOUR, THREE, TWO. . ."

"EVERYBODY JUMP!!!!"

"ONE. . ."

KKKKAAABBBBOOOOOOMMMMM!!!!

We could feel the heat from the explosion behind us as we jumped off the ledge toward our doom.

The flames licked our backs as the entire Mansion **EXPLODED** in a bright red and yellow flame.

I just remember my life flashing before our eyes as I looked to my right and left and saw my mom, dad, Steve, the guys, I.P. and his pinky, Team Cube, Nate, the Street Kids, and all the Pixelmon.

And I just looked down at little Pixelchu in my arms, and closed my eyes. . .

# TUESDAY

The End.

No, I'm serious. . .it would've been the end if it wasn't for that Totem of Undying.

Right before we hit the ground, the Totem started spinning and **GLISTENING** and flashing and next thing you know, we were all okay.

Man, I love Minecraft.

. . .Especially all those updates.

But talk about a crazy adventure.

All I know is that I never want to go through that again.

Well, maybe, just to see my parents in leather and spandex again.

Is that weird?

Well, we **RESCUED** all the Pixelmon and brought them back to all the kids in the neighborhood.

Everybody was so happy that they decided to set up a new Pixelmon tournament in a few weeks.

And it turns out, Team Cube wasn't so bad either. It seems they were just under the Evoker's spell.

They're actually pretty normal.

Except for that Ocelot kid. . .he still keeps dropping the mic everywhere he goes.


The Street Kids finally found a **HOME,** too.

It seems after the explosion, Ichabod talked his uncle into turning Woodland Mansion into an orphanage for wayward kids without parents.

Steve's heading the construction project.

And he's got Nate and the other Street Kids helping him out.

You know, my parents have really chilled out too.

They're not **SO STRICT** anymore about chores and homework and stuff.

I think almost losing our lives probably helped them see what was really important in life.

Either that, or there was something about wearing spandex and leather that made my mom and dad feel young again.

And to be honest, almost losing my parents, and seeing those Street Kids, and not to mention seeing how weird Steve can be. . .it really made me appreciate my mom and dad a lot more.

And I'm probably. . .maybe. . .most likely. . .going to try to do what my parents say from now on. . .maybe.

But, don't say anything, because I will never admit to that **IN PUBLIC.**

No, I mean it. . .if anybody asks me, I'll deny every word.

Gotta represent for the cause, you know.

And you're probably wondering what happened to Pixelchu.

Well, he's not with me anymore.

No. . .no. . .it's not what you think.

You see, that Totem of Undying was also good for other stuff too.

Like bringing back Minecraft Mobs from the dead.

Did a better job than Steve's **POTIONS** could ever do.

So Pixelchu is alive and doing really good.

Where is he?

Well, I decided to bring Pixelchu to Professor Spruce.

Yeah, the Professor was really happy to see his little friend, Experiment 115.

I decided to let the Professor keep Pixelchu as long as he would stop calling him Experiment 115.

"His name is Pixelchu," I told Professor Spruce.

"Pikachu?" he said.

"No, Pixelchu."

"Pickle-chu?"

"No, PIXELCHU!"

After a **FEW ZAPS** from Pixelchu, I think he finally got it.


I figured, even though I cared about Pixelchu a lot, I probably wouldn't be able to keep him away from my mom's cake for very long. Also, my mom is still not happy about the big hole where our kitchen used to be.

So, to prevent any rifts in the **TRANS DIMENSIONAL** universe or any rifts between my mom and me, I thought Pixelchu would be safer with Professor Spruce.

Not to mention, it would probably be safer for the rest of Minecraft World and for the universe as we know it.

So, Pixelchu, I'm going to miss you.

But, I will never forget you.

And you will always be my friend.

Pat. . .Pat. . .

ZZZZAAAAAAPPP!!!!

# FRIDAY

"Hey, Steve!"

"Wassup up, Zombie?"

"Nuthin'. **WASSUP** with you?"

"Nuthin'. Wassup with you?"

"Uh. . .Nuthin'. Wassup with you?"

"Just punching a tree. Hey, what day is it today?"

"I think it's Friday," I said.

"Friday the what?" Steve asked.

"It's Friday the 13th. Why?"

# "FRIDAY THE 13th?!!!! NO WAY!"

I could tell from Steve's face turning a really bright shade of white that something really bad was going to happen.

It's not every day you can scare the bravest guy in Minecraft.

So, I know we're in for another crazy, zany, silly, goofy, wacky, madcap Minecraft Adventure.

Coming soon. . .

# FIND OUT
# WHAT HAPPENS
# NEXT!

## FRIDAY NIGHT FRIGHTS

It's **Friday the 13th** and **Herobrine** is on a mission to **destroy Steve** and All of Minecraft.

But can Zombie and his friends **HELP STEVE OVERCOME** this epic battle? Or, will they get in even more trouble as they embark on another **HILARIOUS MINECRAFT ADVENTURE?**

Made in the USA
Middletown, DE
19 December 2020